Patter-Paws the Squirrel
and other stories

Brien Masters

illustrated by
Brian Gold

TEMPLE LODGE
London

First readers are controversial. Recent educational psychological research has revealed that induced early learning can result in stress and academic disadvantages, even for those children who appear to take it 'in their stride'. This research corroborates educationalist Rudolf Steiner's advice with regard to the teaching of writing and reading. The present volume, taking this advice into account, is primarily intended for use in parallel with the telling of fables as described very specifically in the Waldorf school approach to education. Thus, familiarity with the story, as much as its lively content, is a pre-requisite to the reading process in helping to stimulate the child's interest and hence the necessary motivation and inner momentum.

Within the limits of an early reader, the style adopted has a certain 'literary' quality, one of its distinctive features being the introduction of more advanced phonic structures and letter-patterns—through the proper nouns, nearly all of which are included in the individual titles—simultaneously with simpler and more orthodox progressions of word structures and sound sequences. This is with the intention of building up the child's confidence, thus leading, encouraging and adding leaven to the more disciplined work, with its inevitable more solid pace. The stories are graded according to these principles, together with others such as repetitions in plenty, rhyming devices, a liberal smattering of those common words that form the foundation of 'sight vocabulary' within the language (e.g. said, one) and a carefully structured use of vowels and dipthongs. Two further devices have been incorporated as facilitators; the exclusion of quotation marks and the inclusion of a few out-of-date hyphens.

The child's strong visual sense has also been taken into account: the earlier illustrations depict a moment towards the beginning of each story, so that the child gets away to a good start; the later illustrations portray incidents nearer the end, thus providing a goal to achieve rather than a rousing send-off! The visual element has also been considered in the lay-out, with larger type-face and smaller paragraphs to begin with, in order to whet the appetite, moving through aperitif to main-course size as the young reader's forces of 'print-digestion' gain strength.

(The Author)

First edition 1992

© Brien Masters
Illustrations © Brian Gold

A catalogue record for this book is available from the British Library.

ISBN 0 904693 35 X

Typeset by DP Photosetting, Aylesbury, Bucks
Printed and bound in Great Britain by
The Cromwell Press Limited, Broughton Gifford, Wiltshire

Contents

Patter-Paws the Fox and Sharp-Claws the Lobster

One day Patter-Paws the fox met Sharp-Claws the lobster.

Let's have a race, said Patter-Paws the fox.

Yes let's, said Sharp-Claws the lobster.

They stood side by side.

As they stood side by side they counted: one, two, three. And the race began.

Patter-Paws the fox ran fast, but Sharp-Claws the lobster held tightly onto the fox's tail.

When Patter-Paws the fox had run to the end of the race, Sharp-Claws the lobster let go of the fox's tail.

O, there you are at last, said Sharp-Claws the lobster. Let's have another race.

Patter-Paws the fox panted. When he saw the lobster by his side, he couldn't believe his eyes.

Another race! he panted. No thanks!

And that was the last time that Patter-Paws the fox and Sharp-Claws the lobster met to have a race.

Bushy-Tail the Fox and Long-Beak the Crane

One day Bushy-Tail the Fox asked Long-Beak the Crane along to supper.

Thank you, said Long-Beak the Crane.

The day came. Supper time came. And along came Bushy-Tail the Fox and Long-Beak the Crane.

Bushy-Tail the Fox served soup for supper. He served the soup in a shallow dish. The soup smelt good.

Long-Beak the Crane bent over the shallow soup dish. She tapped and tapped and tapped and tapped with her long beak. But however much she tapped in the shallow dish, she only got soup on the very tip of her long beak. So Bushy-Tail the fox lapped and lapped till all the soup was gone.

A few days later Long-Beak the Crane asked Bushy-Tail the Fox along to supper.

The day came. Supper time came. And along came Long-Beak the Crane and Bushy-Tail the Fox.

9

For supper, Long-Beak the Crane served a delicious drink. She served the delicious drink in a tall, narrow-necked jug. The delicious drink smelt good.

Bushy-Tail the Fox bent over the tall, narrow-necked jug. He stretched his tongue into the narrow neck. He stretched and stretched and stretched and stretched. But however much he stretched he only got the very tip of his tongue wet. So Long-Beak the Crane sipped and sipped till all the delicious drink was gone.

And since then Long-Beak the Crane and Bushy-Tail the Fox haven't ever had supper together again.

The Uncomplaining Oxen and the Creaking Axles

One hot day six oxen were pulling an ox-cart. Up hill and down dale the oxen pulled it, plodding on, uncomplaining. Uncomplaining, they plodded over deep dry ruts and deep fords.

Soon the axles started to creak. They creaked and squeaked. At every rut they creaked and squeaked. At every ford they creaked and squeaked. And at every bump they creaked and squeaked.

But the uncomplaining oxen plodded on.

Hey, complained the first axle, I'm getting dizzy!
Hey, complained the second axle, I'm getting dizzy!
Hey, complained the third axle, I'm getting dizzy!
And, Hey, complained the fourth axle, I'm getting dizzy!

But the uncomplaining oxen still plodded on.

Ouch, creaked the first axle as the cart went over a bump, what a load!
Ouch, creaked the second axle as the cart went over another bump, what a load!
Ouch, creaked the third axle as the cart went over another bump, what a load!

And, Ouch, creaked the fourth axle as the cart went over yet another bump, what a load!

But the uncomplaining oxen just plodded on.

Ow, squeaked the first axle, will the road never end?
Ow, squeaked the second axle, will the road never end?
Ow, squeaked the third axle, will the road never end?
And Ow, squeaked the fourth axle, will the road never end?

But the six uncomplaining oxen kept plodding on.

Why do you dreary oxen never speak to us? complained the first axle again.
Why do you dreary oxen never speak to us? complained the second axle again.
Why do you dreary oxen never speak to us? complained the third axle again.
And, why do you dreary oxen never speak to us? complained the fourth axle again.

But the six uncomplaining oxen still went plodding on.

Relax can't you! squeaked and creaked the first axle as the oxen pulled the cart out of a deep rut.
Relax can't you! squeaked and creaked the second axle as the oxen pulled the cart out of another deep rut.

Relax can't you! squeaked and creaked the third axle as the oxen pulled the cart out of another rut.

And, Relax can't you! squeaked and creaked the fourth axle as the oxen pulled the cart out of yet another rut.

But the uncomplaining oxen plodded on up hill and down dale, over ruts and bumps and through fords. They plodded on till they had pulled the ox-cart all the way home.

And as they were nearing home the first axle squeaked at the top of its voice, I shall be so relieved when I've finished with this job!

And I shall be so relieved when I've finished with this job! squeaked the second axle at the top of its voice.

And I shall be so relieved when I've finished with this job! squeaked the third axle at the top of its shrill voice.

And so shall I be relieved when I've fin. . . .

But that's as far as the fourth axle got with its shrill squeaky voice. The oxen had reached home and were standing still.

And all six of them were still uncomplaining.

Thirsty-Crow and the Water Jug

One day Thirsty-Crow spied a water jug. Thirsty-Crow tried to reach the water, but there was so little in the jug that it was out of reach. He tried and tried again but he couldn't reach the water.

And all the time his thirst grew.

Suddenly he knew what to do. He picked up a stone and dropped it into the water. Then he picked up another stone and dropped it in. But he still couldn't reach the water. So he picked up more and more.

With the stones the water rose until Thirsty-Crow could reach it. So he drank, and what a good drink it was.

The Gambolling Fox Cubs
and the Lioness

A fox was playing with her cubs.

The cubs were rolling and gambolling over one another, and they were rolling and gambolling over the fox.

Suddenly they saw a lioness standing there. The fox cubs stopped rolling and gambolling over one another and ran to the fox's side. Then they saw that the lioness also had a cub.

Where are your other cubs? said the fox to the lioness.

My other cubs? said the lioness. I only have one.

Only one cub, said the fox, sneering.

Only one cub, only one, said the fox cubs, chuckling and ready to begin gambolling again.

Yes, said the lioness slowly, only one. But there is no need for sneering or chuckling; it is a lion.

The Pot

One day a man drove a cart along a road. On the cart were lots and lots of pots.

Suddenly, one pot fell off onto the road.

Along came Flitter-the-Fly. Flitter-the-Fly saw the pot in the road and said, Whose house is this? She saw no-one in it so she went in.

Suddenly along came Buzzer-the-Gnat.

Buzzer-the-Gnat also saw the pot in the road and said, Whose house is this?

It is mine, said Flitter-the-Fly, but do come and live with me.

Suddenly along came Twitcher-the-Mouse.

Twitcher-the-Mouse also saw the pot in the road and said, Whose house is this?

It is ours, said Buzzer-the-Gnat and Flitter-the-Fly, but do come and live with us.

Suddenly along came Croaker-the-Frog.

Croaker-the-Frog also saw the pot in the road and said, Whose house is this?

It is ours, said Twitcher-the-Mouse and Buzzer-the-Gnat and Flitter-the-Fly, but do come and live with us.

Suddenly along came Hopper-the-Hare.

Hopper-the-Hare also saw the pot in the road and said, Whose house is this?

It is ours, said Croaker-the-Frog and Twitcher-the-Mouse and Buzzer-the-Gnat and Flitter-the-Fly, but do come and live with us.

Suddenly along came Slinker-the-Fox.

Slinker-the-Fox also saw the pot in the road and said, Whose house is this?

It is ours, said Hopper-the-Hare and Croaker-the-Frog and Twitcher-the-Mouse and Buzzer-the-Gnat and Flitter-the-Fly, but do come and live with us.

Suddenly along came Hungry-Wolf.

Hungry-Wolf also saw the pot in the road and said, Whose house is this?

It is ours, said Slinker-the-Fox and Hopper-the-Hare and Croaker-the-Frog and Twitcher-the-Mouse and Buzzer-the-Gnat and Flitter-the-Fly, but do come and live with us.

At last Bold-Bear came along.

Bold-Bear also saw the pot in the road and said, Whose house might this be?

It is ours, said Hungry-Wolf and Slinker-the-Fox and Hopper-the-Hare and Croaker-the-Frog and Twitcher-the-Mouse and Buzzer-the-Gnat and Flitter-the-Fly. There is no room left for you.

No room left for me, said Bold-Bear, then I will crush the pot. He sat on the pot and crushed it to pieces.

But before Bold-Bear crushed the pot to pieces, away flitted Flitter-the-Fly. Away buzzed Buzzer-the-Gnat. Away twitched Twitcher-the-Mouse. Away croaked Croaker-the-Frog. Away hopped Hopper-the-Hare. Away slunk Slinker-the-Fox. And away went Hungry-Wolf to look for his next meal.

So Bold-Bear sat all alone on the crushed pot pieces. He felt queer.

Slick Fox and Slicker Cat

One day Slick Fox and Slicker Cat met under a high tree by a stream.

Slick Fox put his nose high in the air and said, Just listen: I am so slick with all my tricks.

This week I've stolen a chicken and I got away; I've stolen a pet rabbit and I got away; I've stolen one of the farmer's best hens and I got away; and I've stolen the farmer's fat goose and I'm still on the loose.

Slicker Cat listened. She listened to Slick Fox with his list of tricks. She listened to the stream and she listened to the wind up in the high tree. And as she listened she heard the sound of bounding hounds in the air.

Up into the high tree jumped Slicker Cat.

Slick Fox heard the sound too. As he listened, he put his nose high in the air. But he was afraid.

He heard the cat say from the high tree, Slick Fox, the hounds are bounding by the stream.

But it was too late for Slick Fox to get away from the hounds. The last thing he heard was Slicker Cat in the tree saying, If only you knew the trick of jumping into the high tree! But it is too late! Where are all your slick tricks now?

Fox Quick-on-the-Uptake, Lion Long-in-Tooth and Brown-Brawny-Bear

Lion Long-in-Tooth and Brown-Brawny-Bear were fighting one another. They were fighting one another for the young kid they had both pounced on. They fought and they fought and they fought.

Brown-Brawny-Bear's tooth tore the flesh of Lion Long-in-Tooth. Lion Long-in-Tooth's claws tore the flesh of Brown-Brawny-Bear.

At last their fighting wore both of them out. Lion Long-in-Tooth was worn out and lay down with heaving sides. Brown-Brawny-Bear was worn out and lay down with heaving sides.

Meanwhile, Fox Quick-on-the-Uptake waited. He waited and watched. He watched them fighting. He watched Brown-Brawny-Bear's tooth. He watched Lion Long-in-Tooth's claws. And he waited for his moment. It was the moment when Brown-Brawny-Bear and Lion Long-in-Tooth were worn out and lay down with heaving sides.

Then quickly Fox Quick-on-the-Uptake pounced between them. He pounced on the young kid. He dug his teeth into its flesh and ran off with it in his mouth.

The Wolf in Sheep's Clothing

A wolf was once hungry, very hungry. He howled and he scowled and he prowled, but he couldn't find anything to eat.

So he thought to himself: Now I shall have to go and kill a sheep.

That night he went to the sheep-fold but he found that the sheep were safe inside.

He howled and he scowled and he prowled but he couldn't get inside the sheep-fold.

So he was even more hungry than before.
Next day he thought to himself: I will play a trick.

He found a sheep skin and put it on. With his sheep skin on he went among the sheep just when they were going into the sheep-fold. And he got into the sheep-fold without the shepherd seeing him.

He wanted to howl. He wanted to scowl. He

wanted to prowl, but he had to keep quiet and he had to wait.

When the shepherd has gone, thought the wolf to himself, I will kill as many sheep as I can eat.

But when all the sheep were safe in the sheep-fold, the shepherd strode in with a knife. He wanted to kill a sheep for supper. So he strode into the middle of the sheep-fold.
I will kill this one, thought the shepherd to himself.

It was the wolf in sheep's clothing.

Woolly-eyed Sheep, Sly-eyed Fox and Ravenous-eyed Wolf

Woolly-eyed Sheep always got the blame when ram was naughty. So Woolly-eyed Sheep ran away from home. She followed her nose.

On the way she met Sly-eyed Fox.
Where are you going? he said.
I'm running away from home, following my nose, said Woolly-eyed Sheep. When ram is naughty, I always get the blame.
Same with me, said Sly-eyed Fox. I'm running away from home, following my nose; when hawk takes a little hen, I get the blame.
So they went on together, following their noses.

On the way they met Ravenous-eyed Wolf.
Where are you going? he said.

We're running away from home, following our noses, they said. We're always getting the blame. Woolly-eyed Sheep gets the blame when ram is naughty and I get the blame when hawk takes a little hen said Sly-eyed Fox.

Let's all go together then, said Ravenous-eyed Wolf.
So they did, following their noses.

As they went on, wolf got more and more ravenous.
Woolly-eyed Sheep, he said, you are wearing my fur coat.
At that, Sly-eyed Fox said, Are you sure that it's your fur coat?
Yes, I am sure, certainly, said Ravenous-eyed Wolf.
Will you swear it's yours with a kiss? said Sly-eyed Fox.
Yes certainly, said the wolf.

Let's go together then, said Sly-eyed Fox. Woolly-eyed Sheep and I will watch you swear with a kiss.
Sly-eyed Fox led the wolf to a farmer's trap. All three stood beside the trap.
Here we are, said Sly-eyed Fox, swear with a kiss.
Stupidly, Ravenous-eyed Wolf put his nose into the trap. Snap went the trap, trapping the wolf.

So Woolly-eyed Sheep kept her fur coat. And she and Sly-eyed Fox went off, following their noses.

Busily-Buzzing-the-Gnat and Powerful-Bull

One morning at corn harvest, Busily-Buzzing-the-Gnat came buzzing busily from his cloud of gnats to where Powerful-Bull was grazing, and chewing with his powerful jaw, and gazing with his powerful eye.

Powerful-Bull lifted his powerful neck. He stood with his powerful legs. He chewed with his powerful jaw. He gazed with his powerful eye. But he did not use his powerful voice; he said nothing.

A nice morning, said the gnat as he buzzed round the bull's powerful nose, I hope you are well.
But the bull said nothing.

A nice sunny morning for the corn harvest, said the gnat as he buzzed by the bull's powerful eye.
Still the bull made no reply.

The farmer's wife has torn her apron this morning, buzzed the gnat, as he settled on the bull's powerful neck.

The bull was silent.

The price of pork and beef is going up, buzzed the gnat.
Still no reply.

The farmer said he needs to buy a new torch, Busily-
Buzzing-the-Gnat went as he settled on the bull's powerful
leg.
But still the bull chewed with his powerful jaw but said
nothing.

The gnat settled on the bull's powerful horn: Are you
taking a holiday this year? A short holiday maybe? Maybe
after the corn harvest?

The gnat buzzed on and on in his busy well-worn way
until he said: Powerful-Bull, I hope you don't mind, but I
must be going now.
At last the bull used his powerful voice. I did not notice you
come and will certainly not notice you go, was all he said.

Powerful-Bull went on chewing with his powerful jaw
and gazing with his powerful eye, snorting once with his
powerful nose as Busily-Buzzing-the-Gnat buzzed off – back
to his cloud of gnats, back to his cloud of buzzing.

Thrush-in-the-Bush and Old-Crow-Know-All

One day Old-Crow-Know-All was perched in his favourite tree when along came Thrush-in-the-Bush. Thrush-in-the-Bush perched in his favourite bush and sang his favourite song. It was a lovely song.

I know how to sing that song, said Old-Crow-Know-All and so saying he sang a song as lovely as Thrush-in-the-Bush's. So, perched up in the tree, sang Old-Crow-Know-All and down below, perched in the bush, sang Thrush-in-the-Bush.

As they were singing along came Noddy-the-Horse.
What are you singing? he said to Thrush-in-the-Bush.
I'm singing my favourite song, said Thrush-in-the-Bush, do you sing?
Me, sing? No not I, said the horse.
Noddy-the-Horse rushed off at the trot and as he trotted he neighed. He neighed very loudly.

Old-Crow-Know-All heard how loudly Noddy-the-Horse neighed and he said to Thrush-in-the-Bush: I know how to sing that song.

That isn't a song, said Thrush-in-the-Bush.

It *is* a song, said Old-Crow-Know-All, and I know how to sing it.

And so saying, he started. But it was not singing and it was not lovely. It went, Caw-Caw.

What are you doing? said Thrush-in-the-Bush.

I'm singing like Noddy-the-Horse, said the old crow as he went on with his Caw-Caw.

By this time, Noddy-the-Horse had trotted back.

What are you doing? he said when he saw Old-Crow-Know-All going Caw-Caw.

I'm singing like you, said the crow.

I don't sing like that, said the horse, and so saying he rushed off at the trot and neighed loudly.

Thrush-in-the-Bush on his favourite perch in his favourite bush went on singing his favourite song.

But Old-Crow-Know-All had forgotten how to sing. Perched up in his tree he just went on going, Caw-Caw, Caw-Caw.

Egg-Layer the Hen, Red-Comb the Cockerel and Shady Fox

One day Shady Fox was out for a walk in a shady little wood.

On his walk who should he hear but Red-Comb the Cockerel and Egg-Layer the Hen. Red-Comb the Cockerel and Egg-Layer the Hen were having a little talk. When they saw Shady Fox coming they flew into a tree.

Good day to you both, said Shady Fox with a cunning grin.

Good day to you, said Red-Comb the Cockerel and Egg-Layer the Hen.

Shall we have a little talk? said Shady Fox.

That would be good, said Red-Comb the Cockerel and Egg-Layer the Hen.

Then could you come a little lower down the tree, said the fox, I'm a little deaf today.

Deaf today are you? they said, Oh Dear! And they came a little lower down the tree.

Could you come still lower down the tree, said the fox with a cunning grin.

We could come a little lower, they said but they still kept out of reach.

Still lower? said the cunning fox, It is a day of peace, my dears.

A day of peace is it? said Red-Comb the Cockerel and Egg-Layer the Hen, We hadn't heard of that.

All the same they wouldn't go lower.

We can talk from here, they said.

The cunning old fox begged them to come down but they wouldn't.

Suddenly Red-Comb the Cockerel started to talk to Egg-Layer the Hen: What can you hear from over the hill? he said.

Barking, my dear, I think, said the hen.

Shady Fox pricked up one ear.

What can you see coming over the hill? said Egg-Layer the Hen going on with their little talk.

Hounds, my dear, I think, said he, and their red tongues are hanging out.

Shady Fox pricked up the other ear.

How lovely, my dear, said Red-Comb the Cockerel, I think they are coming this way.

Yes, my dear, said Egg-Layer the Hen, I think they could be coming for the day of peace.

By this time, Shady Fox had heard enough talk. That is enough, he said, it could be that the hounds haven't heard of the day of peace. After all, you hadn't heard of it.

He ran off to save his skin. And with the fox went his cunning grin.

So Red-Comb the Cockerel and Egg-Layer the Hen went on with their little talk in the peace of the shady little wood.

Old-Hound and Wily-Fox

Once there was a farm-worker who lived in a farm-worker's cottage with his wife. They had a hound who was very old. The old hound had a place by the cottage door.

One day the farm-worker said to his wife, I will take the old hound and leave it in the forest. It is no use to us now for it can't work any more.

So the farm-worker put a lead on the hound and led it into the forest. As he went he thought, I will hang the hound.

But when he got deep into the forest he saw tears in the hound's eyes.

At that the farm-worker couldn't bring himself to hang the hound. So he went back to his wife with the lead and left the hound in the forest.

Still with tears in his eyes, the hound lay in the forest alone, when Wily-Fox came by.

Old-Hound, what are you doing here? asked Wily-Fox. You're all alone in the forest.

So the good old hound told the wily fox all the sad story. Wily Fox said, I will help you.

The next day the farm-worker and his wife were going to work in the fields. They were going to make hay. It was a sunny day so they put their things by the hedge. For by the hedge was a cool place for the water bottle. The farm-worker put the water bottle there and his wife said, I will hang the lunch bag on this branch. Then they started to make hay.

Now Old-Hound and Wily-Fox were hiding behind the hedge. From behind the hedge they watched the farm-worker and his wife. Wily-Fox watched from one end of the hay field and Old-Hound watched from the other end.

Suddenly Wily-Fox came out from behind the hedge. He ran into the field and snatched down the lunch bag.

The farm-worker and his wife saw Wily-Fox. They saw him snatch the lunch bag and run across the field. Old-Hound also saw the fox snatch the lunch bag and run across the field. Then Old-Hound saw the farmer and his wife chase Wily-Fox with their hay rakes. They chased him round and round the field.

Still Old-Hound watched. He watched as Wily-Fox came

nearer and nearer. Then suddenly the hound also came out from behind the hedge. He snatched the lunch bag from Wily-Fox and ran with it to the farm-worker and his wife.

They put down their hay rakes. They took the lunch bag from Old-Hound and patted him. And as they patted him they said, Good old hound. You saved our lunch bag. You must come and live with us again in our cottage.

Old-Hound now had tears of joy in his eyes. He wanted to thank Wily-Fox for all his help, but Wily-Fox was far too wily to hang around where there were hay rakes.

Vain-Crow and Flattering-Fox

Vain-Crow had found a piece of cheese one day. With the cheese in his beak he flew onto the branch of a tree.

Along came Flattering-Fox.

Cheese! He could smell cheese!

He saw Vain-Crow on the tree branch, and in his beak he could see what he could smell: cheese.

Your beautiful feathers are well preened today, said Flattering-Fox with a foxy smile.

Vain-Crow stretched his neck and shook his beautiful, preened feathers a little but said nothing.

Your wings are beautiful against the blue sky today, flattered the fox, with his foxy smile again.

Vain-Crow spread his beautiful wings a little and looked up at the blue sky, but said nothing.

I would love to hear one of your beautiful songs, flattered the fox again.

Vain-Crow stretched his neck a little and opened his beak to sing. But before he could sing the cheese fell out.

A lost piece of cheese is not much to sing about, said the crow to himself, as Flattering-Fox chewed the cheese – still with his foxy smile.

Slick-Slipper the Goose and Lip-Licker the Fox

One day Slick-Slipper the Goose was waddling on the shore of a lake. She was a fine fat goose.

As she was waddling, Lip-Licker the Fox hid close by, behind a thick patch of thistles. He was licking his lips. Still licking his lips, he crept closer. But he still hid behind the thick patch of thistles.

Suddenly he had her in his mouth.

She hissed and she cackled, she cackled and she struggled, she struggled and she hissed. But she could not get out of his mouth.

So Lip-Licker the fox teased Slick-Slipper the Goose.

Aha, he said, I'm not going to let you loose.

The goose cackled and hissed, she hissed and struggled, she struggled and cackled.

He teased her again. If I were in your mouth, what would you do now? he said.

Quickly Slick-Slipper the Goose said, I would close my eyes and say grace before my meal, so that you would taste better.

Taste better? said the fox, that's a good idea.

He put Slick-Slipper the Goose down, closed his eyes, licked his lips once more and started to say grace.

But no sooner had he started to say grace than the goose slipped slickly away and was quickly swimming across the lake.

Lip-Licker the Fox was amazed. He had no goose in his mouth any more. He was simply amazed. He gazed across the lake in amazement. He licked his lips in amazement. And as he licked his lips he was amazed to taste goose. But it was only the tiniest taste of goose-feather. He licked his lips in amazement and disgust.

The tiniest taste of goose-feather does not make a meal.

Branching-Antlers the Stag

One night Branching-Antlers the Stag stood beside a lake. The night was bright with moon-light.

Beside the lake, the stag looked into the water. He saw the moon in the water. He saw himself in the water. He saw his branching antlers in the water. And on his branching antlers fell moon-light, bright moon-light.

How beautiful I look in the water, said the stag to himself. How beautiful my branching antlers look in the moon-light.

All night he kept looking at his branching antlers thinking how beautiful they were in the moon-light.

The night passed and day came. The moon set and sun-rise filled the sky. The air was filled with morning light, but it was also filled with the hunter's horn and the barking of hounds.

The horn and the barking hounds came nearer and nearer to the lake. Branching-Antlers-the-Stag heard the sound of hound and horn filling the air.

The stag started to run. He ran swiftly. He looked for shelter.

The trees will give shelter, he said to himself. Swiftly he ran into the shelter of the trees. Swiftly the barking hounds ran, sniffing the air.

Suddenly the stag could run no longer. His branching antlers were stuck in the twigs of the trees. He pulled and twisted his beautiful head. But it was no good. The antlers were stuck in the branches of the trees.

The hunter's horn filled the air as the hounds pounced on the stag. The hunter's hounds brought the stag to the ground. To the ground they brought the beautiful stag. To the ground they brought his beautiful head and to the ground fell his beautiful antlers.

Greedy Dog and Juicy Bone

One day Greedy Dog had a bone. The bone had some juicy meat on it. Greedy Dog took the juicy bone in his mouth to where he could eat it alone.

On the way he had to cross a bridge. The bridge went across a deep, still pond. On the bridge Greedy Dog looked into the deep, still pond. And in the pond he saw a dog. The dog had a juicy bone in its mouth.

That bone is juicy, thought Greedy Dog to himself. It is more juicy than my bone and has more meat on it than mine. I will grab it.

Greedy Dog opened his mouth to grab it. As he did so, the dog in the pond opened his mouth too. There was a splash. The deep pond was no longer still.

Greedy Dog waited until the pond was still again. He still wanted to grab the juicy bone from the dog he had seen in the pond. He still thought of the juicy meat.

I will grab it in my mouth and eat it all alone, he thought greedily to himself.

But when the pond was still again, the bone had vanished – meat, juice and all.

Furtive-Fox and Gullible-Goat

One day Furtive-Fox fell into a well. The well was deep but it was dry. The well was too deep for Furtive-Fox to jump out.

Along came Gullible-Goat. Gullible-Goat was dry with thirst. Gullible-Goat saw the deep well.

From inside the well Furtive-Fox called out to Gullible-Goat.

Who is calling? said Gullible Goat.

I am calling, replied Furtive-Fox.

Where are you? said Gullible-Goat.

I am here in the well, replied Furtive-Fox, come and help me out.

How can I help you out? said Gullible-Goat.

Jump into the well here, replied Furtive-Fox, and I will jump onto your back and climb out. Then I will help you climb out.

Gullible-Goat jumped in. He stretched out his front legs, up to the brim of the well.

Furtive-Fox jumped onto Gullible-Goat's back and climbed out of the well.

Help me out now, said Gullible Goat.

But there was no reply. Furtive-Fox had run away.

Lusty-Lion and Trusty-Mouse

Trusty-Mouse lived near Lusty-Lion.

One day Trusty-Mouse got trapped. He was trapped in the lion's paw.

Now I will eat you, you little scamp, roared Lusty-Lion as he opened wide his lusty jaw.

Don't do that, squeaked Trusty-Mouse, and one day I will help you.

You help me! roared Lusty-Lion with a smile. You little scamp. And he snapped again with his jaw.

Please, squeaked the mouse.

So the lion opened his paw and let Trusty-Mouse go free. Off he scampered as he squeaked. Thank you Lusty-Lion.

Some days later Lusty-Lion himself got trapped. He was trapped in the huntsman's net. He roared with anger.

Trusty-Mouse heard the lion's roar. He came to the trap and squeaked: Hello.

Is that you Trusty-Mouse? roared the lion, Look at this net of rope.

Trusty-Mouse scampered down the slope to the huntsman's rope trap and started to nibble. He nibbled and nibbled with his trusty sharp teeth.

Suddenly, the rope snapped. Lusty-Lion was free. He shook his lusty paw. He shook his lusty mane. He lashed his lusty tail.

Thank you, Trusty-Mouse he roared. You scamp!

Good-bye Lusty-Lion, squeaked the mouse. And off he scampered.